This Book Is A Gift From

LINDA KEMMERER

AUGUST 2003

©Highsmith® Inc. 1999

Slonker's Lucky Day

Kipchak Johnson

Published by
LAZY SUMMER BOOKS
16 St Margaret's Road
Oxford OX2 6RU
© 1984 Lazy Summer Books
ISBN 0 946801 00 2

Printed in Belgium by Henri Proost, Turnhout, Belgium.

"Get out! Get out!" shouted Mrs Badger to her son, Slonker. "You're the laziest, grumpiest young badger in the wood. You never help in the hole. You never bring me any nuts or roots. You're so lazy you just lie around daydreaming — and yet you eat twice as much as anybody!"

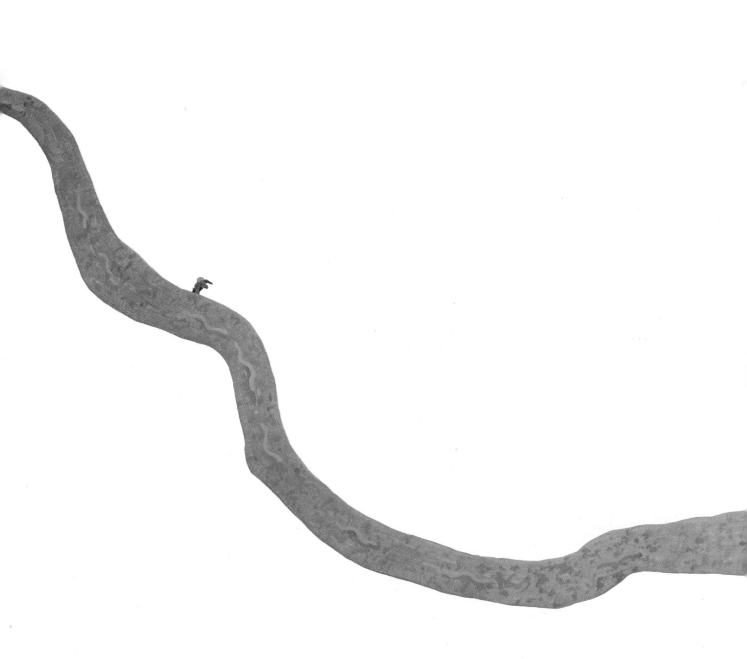

"I need to eat more", Slonker replied. "I'm growing aren't I?"

"Growing fatter and lazier," said his mother. "You're too old to be daydreaming all day. You must get a job and earn some money. There's plenty of jobs in the wood for a healthy young badger."

Slonker shuddered. A boring job in the wood — ugh! The thought of it made him feel sick. He dreamt he would be rich and famous when he grew up, and he did not want to have an ordinary job in the wood.

"Well, I've had enough of you," continued Mrs Badger. "If you won't look for a job, you'll have to leave the hole. But daydreams won't get you far in the big, wide world — you'll soon find out!"

Later in the day, where the road to London passes a corner of Badger Wood, a rather miserable young badger left the shelter of the trees, scrambled clumsily through the hedge and set off down the road. On his back he carried a haversack which contained an old cup and a slice of acorn pie.

Slonker Badger had left home.

He walked a long way. The sun was hot, and he was starting to feel tired when he came to a roadside café. There were several lorries parked outside and a car — a remarkably shiny and splendid Rolls Royce with tinted windows.

"Ah," he thought, "perhaps someone here can give me a lift."

Inside the café was noisy, steamy and full of lorry drivers. Opposite the door sat a man wearing the grey cap and uniform of a chauffeur.

"Excuse me," said Slonker, "can you give me a lift in your car?"

"Why sure," answered the man.

They walked out of the café to the shiny Rolls Royce.

"You get in the back," said the chauffeur, opening the door for him.

Slonker pushed his haversack onto the seat and climbed in, but before he had time to settle himself, a loud voice said;

"*Oh no*, James! What have you found this time? I mean, what is this *creature* that you found in the café? Is it a *bear* or something?"

Slonker shrank into his corner of the back seat. He was so astonished he had no time to notice the expensive plush leather seats, the gold embossed telephone or the bottle of lemonade and the glasses on the little table. For he was facing the *strangest* looking animal — a poodle whose head had been shaved entirely bald apart from a few spikes of bright green fur.

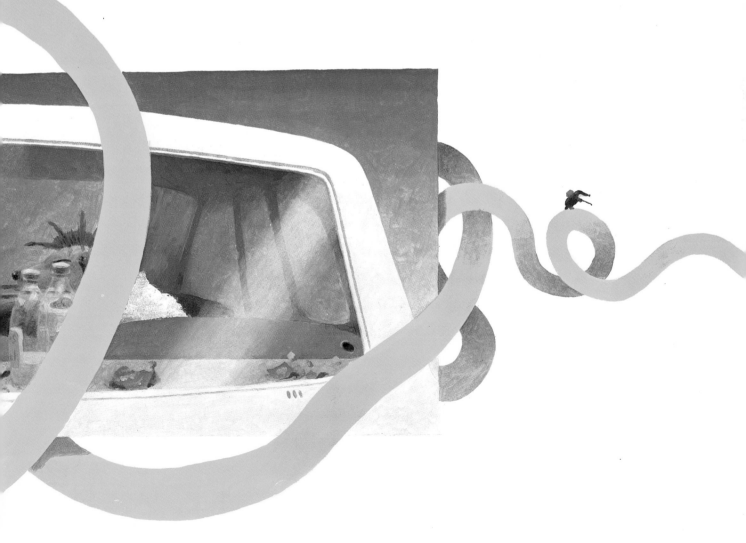

He stared at Slonker rudely, then reached forward and poured himself a lemonade with a well brushed paw.

"Well?" he said, "speak up — what sort of animal are you?"

Slonker searched for something to say, but somehow all his words had run away and hidden themselves.

"Can't you speak?" The poodle leant towards him. "Perhaps you could give me a little grunt — just to sort of let me know you're *alive*, if you know what I mean."

Slonker stared back silently.

"Well if you don't speak and you don't grunt, what can you do?" the poodle enquired. He took a swig of lemonade, then sat up suddenly. "All right, I'll try to guess what kind of animal you are. OK?"

He added a slice of lemon to his glass and then, as the car swung onto the road, he shouted;

"SKUNK!"

"There's no need for that kind of talk," said the chauffeur, glancing in the mirror.

"It's a *game,*" the poodle answered, "just a game, see?"

"I'm a badger," Slonker managed finally.

"Wow," said the poodle, "a badger!"

He made it sound wonderful and unusual. Slonker had always thought of himself as a very ordinary sort of animal. Now he started to feel rather pleased with himself.

"My name's Shimmerin' Stephen," continued the poodle. "I'm lead singer of the Quadrupeds, the world famous pop group — you've probably heard of me." He stuck out his paw.

At that moment the phone rang.

Shimmerin' Stephen reached over and lifted the phone from its cradle. An excited voice crackled down the line. After a short conversation he slammed the phone back, and said:

"Wow, man!"

"Do you mean *bow-wow,* or just wow?" asked the chauffeur.

"I mean *wow,* man — wow, Wow, WOW!" answered the poodle.

There was silence while the chauffeur steered past a lorry.

"Well?" said the poodle, "are you going to ask me what that phone call was about?"

"Yeah," answered the chauffeur, easing the car back into the middle lane of the road.

"That was my agent on the phone," announced the poodle. "He says we're to play on Top of the Pops, the chart topping television programme — and it's tonight! We must be at the television studio by five o'clock — so drive fast!" he added, throwing himself triumphantly back in his seat.

"We'll never make it to London by five o'clock," replied the chauffeur.

"We will if you drive fast. So step on it — go, Go, GO!"

With a surge of power the Rolls Royce cut forward, leaping past the ordinary traffic like a wonderful race horse. Slonker was forced back into the rich leather of his seat.

Then the phone rang again.

After another hurried conversation the poodle slammed the phone back onto its cradle, and said;

" *Wow*, man," but this time with an unhappy, downwards note.

"Yeah?" asked the chauffeur.

"It's Bill, our drummer," answered the poodle. "He's broken his tail, he's in hospital."

"Can't he get *out* of hospital?"

"No he can't. They've put the tail in traction. There's no way he can be with us on the television show tonight."

The poodle poured himself another glass of lemonade, then slumped dejectedly.

"Can't you appear on the show without him?" asked the chauffeur.

"No way. We've got to have a drummer: we're that sort of pop group — we need those drums!"

All this while Slonker had sat quietly, trying not to look out of the window at the lorries which slipped past at a terrifying speed. The soft comfort of his seat made him feel sleepy. He closed his eyes and tried to imagine he was the owner of this fast car, on his way to appear on a television show of his own.

"Hey, you!"

He opened his eyes and his pleasant day dream was shattered by the sight of the poodle's head with the spikes of bright green fur. It was shoved close to his own.

"I've been thinking," said the poodle. "Perhaps *you* could drum — just for the one occasion?"

"Well I ..."

"Sure, man, there's nothing to it." As Slonker retreated the poodle followed him into the corner of the seat. "You just take the drum sticks and — bang, bang, bang — there you are!"

"But I never ..."

"Well that's settled then," said the poodle in a determined tone of voice. " have a glass of lemonade."

Meanwhile the car had turned onto the motorway. Now it rushed down the fast lane, passing cars and lorries as if they were donkey carts.

" *Oh no*, man!" said the chauffeur.

"What do you mean — *oh no*, man?" asked the poodle.

The chauffeur kept glancing in the car mirror. "It's the police," he said.

"Well, can't you go any faster?"

"No way. We're way over the speed limit already," said the chauffeur. "We're doing a hundred miles an hour as it is."

"Well do some more then!" The poodle looked cross.

There was another surge of power. They watched the speedometer creep up; first to a hundred and ten then to a hundred and twenty and finally to a hundred and thirty miles an hour. Slonker dug his claws into the back of the driving seat . His mouth was dry.

But although they were racing so fast, the police car crept closer and closer. Soon it was just behind them and its blue light cast strange shadows across the inside of the Rolls Royce.

"FASTER, FASTER!" shrieked the poodle.

The chauffeur took out his handkerchief and dabbed his forehead.

"I don't know why we're racing along like this," he replied. "We'll never get to the television studio on time — even if we go two hundred miles an hour."

Then all of a sudden they heard a loud, harsh voice calling to them above the roar of the engine.

"STOP AT THE SIDE OF THE MOTORWAY," it called. "PULL IN TO THE SIDE OF THE MOTORWAY." Oddly it seemed to come from just above the car roof.

The poodle wound down his window and leant out.

"There's a police helicopter flying just above the car," he announced, peering upwards. "They're talking to us through a loud speaker."

"We're done for," said the chauffeur. "We can't race a helicopter."

"Are helicopters *much* faster than cars?" asked the poodle, a thoughtful expression on his face.

" *Much* faster."

"Then I'll go by helicopter."

"Don't talk crazy," the chauffeur told him.

"STOP AT THE SIDE OF THE MOTORWAY," the voice ordered again . "STOP AT ONCE!"

"Stop at nothing!" shouted the poodle.

"Don't!" called Slonker.

But the poodle had started to squeeze out of the car window.

"Oh dear," thought Slonker. "The excitement has clearly been too much for him. He's gone mad — I must stop him." He caught hold of one of the poodle's hind legs and gripped it firmly.

Next moment both poodle and leg shot upwards through the car window — and Slonker with them.

The poodle had caught hold of the bottom of the helicopter just as it started to climb into the sky. Soon they were far above the roof of the Rolls Royce. A fierce wind tugged at Slonker's fur and forced its way up his nose.

His arm had just started to ache really horribly from holding onto the poodle's hind leg, when a policeman's hand appeared through the door of the helicopter. It caught hold of the poodle and lifted them both to safety.

"You're under arrest for driving dangerously," the policeman told them as soon as they were safe inside. He produced a pair of handcuffs and locked their wrists together.

The poodle said nothing, but a wild, mad look had come into his eyes. He stared at the microphone for the loudspeaker, which lay on the floor beside the policeman's foot.

It was not long before the helicopter dipped towards a modern building beside the motorway.

"We're about to land at the police station," said the policeman.

At that moment the poodle leapt to his feet and grabbed the microphone from the floor.

"CALLING ALL ANIMALS! CALLING ALL ANIMALS!" he shouted into it, and his voice boomed from the loudspeaker outside the helicopter. It echoed across the motorway and the fields beyond.

"Give that back!" said the policeman angrily.

The poodle only growled and shouted again:

"CALLING ALL ANIMALS! CALLING ALL ANIMALS!"

Through the trap door Slonker saw a dog look up at them. Then there was a little bump and the helicopter came to rest on the roof of the police station.

"CALLING ALL ANIMALS! GATHER ROUND!" shouted the poodle.

Two police dogs and a cat ran across the station yard towards them. The policeman made a grab for the microphone, but the poodle nipped between his legs.

"CALLING ALL ANIMALS! HELP US PLEASE!

DOGS AND CATS AND MICE AND GEESE!" he shouted.

Five police dogs, three cats, ten pigeons and a horse had appeared beneath them in the station yard.

"CALLING ALL ANIMALS! HELP US PLEASE!
RAT AND BAT AND WILDEBEEST!
ELEPHANT AND POLAR BEAR
TINY SHREW AND WILD MARCH HARE!"

Ten police dogs, seven cats, twenty pigeons, the horse and a goat gazed up at them.

"FROM FARM OR FIELD OR LONDON ZOO
THIS IS SHIMMERIN' STEPHEN CALLING YOU!"

shouted the poodle.

The policeman stopped chasing him.

"Excuse me," he said, "did you say Shimmerin' Stephen?"

The poodle looked at him coldly.

"That's right," he answered.

"Do you mean — Shimmerin' Stephen, lead singer of the Quadrupeds, the world famous pop group?" asked the policeman.

There was now a large crowd of animals below the helicopter. "We want Stephen! We want Stephen!" they called.

"That's me," said the poodle.

"Hey, George," the policeman called to the pilot of the helicopter, "we've arrested Shimmerin' Stephen lead singer of the Quadrupeds!"

"Wow!" said the pilot.

"Do you mean *the* Shimmerin' Stephen," the policeman continued, "the one who sings ...?"

"That's me, man," the poodle answered, "and this is Slonker our new drummer. We're on our way to record a session of Top of the Pops, the chart topping television programme, and if you don't hurry up and let us go, we shall be late!"

"Oh wow, man," said the policeman. "I mean — that would be *terrible*! We all love your music at the police station. If you'll just hold on one minute, sir, while I discuss this with the pilot ..."

Half a minute later he was back.

"We've decided," he said, "to overlook your offence in driving too fast and breaking the speed limit. And because we're special fans of yours, we'll take you to the television studio ourselves."

Once more they rose into the air. Below them the animals called louder than ever:

"We want Stephen! We want Stephen!"

The poodle looked sad.

"I've called them together, and now I'm going away without singing to them," he said. He lifted the microphone to his lips.

"SO LONG FANS," he shouted into it. "THANK YOU FOR COMING ROUND — AND WATCH ME ON THE TELEVISION SCREEN TONIGHT!"

The helicopter picked up speed. Soon fields gave way to factories and blocks of flats. The tangled streets of London sped past beneath them, and they were in the centre of the city, skimming over long lines of rush hour traffic. Then there it was — Bush House, home of television!

It was a large, brightly lit building. They landed outside the main entrance and, before they had entirely stopped, uniformed attendants rushed to open the doors of the helicopter.

It was all "This way please, sir" and "May I take your bag, sir?" Slonker was hustled down a long corridor. In front of him the poodle started to sway and click his fingers, calling out to friends in the various dressing rooms. Go-go girls rushed past them and disc jockeys carrying lists of hit records.

Then Slonker was in the make-up room, in a reclining chair with his feet up. In front of him a mirror surrounded by coloured lights.

"What shall I do with this one?" asked the make-up girl. She stood over him with a comb and a pair of scissors.

"Shave his head and dye the rest of him blue!" called the poodle from the next door chair.

"Not *blue,* man!" said a deep voice.

Looking to his left, Slonker saw a large dalmation dog with his fur in curlers. His claws had been painted with purple nail varnish.

"He ought to be yellow," the dalmation continued, "I can *feel* it."

"Dye his head orange and shave the rest of him!" called another voice and, looking beyond the dalmation, Slonker saw a spaniel whose fur had been dyed a violent, shocking pink.

"No, No, NO!" Slonker shouted suddenly. He stood up proudly from his chair. "I am a *badger* ."

"We know that," the poodle said soothingly, "of *course* you're a badger. We just want you to look good, that's all."

"Yeah sure," agreed the dalmation. "We're thinking of you, kid."

"How about stripes?" suggested the Spaniel. "Badgers have stripes, don't they ?"

Half an hour later the three original members of the Quadruped pop group, followed by Slonker, burst onto the stage of the Top of the Pops studio. A pair of smooth, new drum sticks had been thrust into Slonker's hand. When the music started they seemed to dance across the drums with a life of their own. It was easy as picking acorns — easier! Slonker was a natural drummer.

The audience went wild! They loved the way the poodle sang, the way the dalmation danced round the stage and the way the spaniel wiggled his hips — but best of all they liked the new drummer. And when the song was finished all anyone could talk about was Slonker.

"Wow , man," said a goat in the front row, "he's fantastic!"

"Yeah!"

So Slonker's dreams came true. From that day he grew rich and famous.

"But," said his mother, when he drove back to visit her in his own big shiny car, with lots of lovely presents in the boot. "I'd much rather you had stayed here and helped me look after the hole."

"But you told me to get out," he answered.

"Yes, dear," she said, "but I didn't *mean* it — not really!"

So he gave her the biggest present in the pile.